P9-CEH-275

Turkey
Trouble

This book belongs to

MRS

NEWMAN

YEARLING BOOKS are designed especially to entertain and enlighten young people. Patricia Reilly Giff, consultant to this series, received her bachelor's degree from Marymount College and a master's degree in history from St. John's University. She holds a Professional Diploma in reading and a Doctorate of Humane Letters from Hofstra University. She was a teacher and reading consultant for many years, and is the author of numerous books for young readers.

A POLK STREET SPECIAL

TURKEY TROUBLE

. . .

Patricia Reilly Giff

Illustrated by Blanche Sims

A YEARLING BOOK

Published by
Bantam Doubleday Dell Books for Young Readers
a division of
Bantam Doubleday Dell Publishing Group, Inc.
1540 Broadway
New York, New York 10036

If you purchased this book without a cover you should
be aware that this book is stolen property. It was reported as
"unsold and destroyed" to the publisher and neither the
author nor the publisher has received any payment
for this "stripped book."

Text copyright © 1994 by Patricia Reilly Giff

Illustrations copyright © 1994 by Blanche Sims

All rights reserved. No part of this book may be reproduced
or transmitted in any form or by any means, electronic or
mechanical, including photocopying, recording, or by any
information storage and retrieval system, without the
written permission of the Publisher, except where
permitted by law.

The trademarks Yearling® and Dell® are registered in the U.S.
Patent and Trademark Office and in other countries.

ISBN: 0-440-40955-1

Printed in the United States of America

Book Design by Christine Swirnoff

November 1994

10 9 8 7 6

CWO

Love to our own Thanksgiving baby:

Caitlin Patricia Giff
November 17, 1993

Chapter 1

Emily Arrow marched down the street.

She had to march slowly.

She was carrying doubles of everything.

Spellers and notebooks.

Homework pads.

And two bags of Mr. Mancina's Marvelous Popcorn Mix.

Emily rang Dawn Bosco's front bell.

Inside, she could hear feet tap-tapping down the stairs.

"Coming," someone called.

It was Noni, Dawn's grandmother.

She opened the door. "Emily Arrow with Dawn's homework," she said. "Come in."

Emily followed Noni inside. She could hear the television blaring in the living room.

Noni smiled. "Did the new baby come yet?"

Emily shook her head. "Soon."

Dawn was lying on the couch. She popped her head up. "I'm still sick. But don't worry. It's not catching."

"It's too much eating candy," said Noni. "That whole Halloween bag . . . licorice, and candy corn, and peanuts, and raisins, and—"

"Stop," Dawn said. "I don't want to think about food."

Emily handed a bag of Mr. Mancina's mix to Dawn. "Sorry. It's from the principal. A November present."

Dawn closed her eyes. She put the bag on the table next to her. "I can't even look at it," she said.

Emily handed her the homework next. "I'm supposed to tell you about the Thanksgiving Feast."

"Tell her sitting down," said Noni.

Emily slid into a chair. "We're going to have a feast for the kindergartners . . . and for us, too."

Dawn moaned. "Don't . . ."

Emily rushed on. "Ms. Rooney is making a turkey and—"

"Don't say another word about—"

"Sorry," Emily said again. "There's a no-food part."

"Good," said Dawn.

"We're supposed to wear Thanksgiving costumes," Emily said.

She swallowed.

Matthew was going to be Squanto.

Beast was going to be a Pilgrim father.

Jill was going to be a Pilgrim mother.

Emily was the only one without a costume.

Dawn sat up straight. "I think I'll be an Indian princess," she said. "I have a costume with fringe . . . a headband with beads."

Dawn leaned back against the pillow again. "Gorgeous," she said.

That Dawn was the luckiest girl in the world, Emily thought.

She watched Dawn's cat from the corner of her eye.

The cat had jumped up on the table.

She was pushing at the bag with one paw.

"What will you be, Emily?" Noni asked.

"I don't have . . ." Emily began.

"You have that pumpkin costume," Dawn said.

"That's Halloween," Emily said.

At that moment Noni spotted the cat.

She grabbed for her.

Too late.

The cat batted the bag off the table.

Popcorn, and Wheat Chex, and cheese bits scattered all over the floor.

Noni bent over to pick them up.

Emily bent over to help.

Noni looked up at Dawn. "You have an extra costume."

Dawn shook her head. "I don't think so."

"You certainly do," said Noni. "A Pilgrim dress."

"Maybe," Dawn said. She frowned at Noni.

Emily sat up straight.

Terrific.

So what if Jill was going to be a Pilgrim mother?

Why not two Pilgrim mothers?

"I'll have to think," Dawn said. "Maybe I can remember where I put it."

"Think hard," Noni said, staring at Dawn.

Emily crossed her fingers. "Yes, think hard," she said.

Chapter 2

Emily drew a picture of a girl in a Pilgrim dress.

A beautiful girl.

She looked again.

The girl looked like a hippopotamus.

Emily was the worst artist in the world.

She began to erase.

Eraser dots flew all over the place.

She brushed them off with her sleeve.

Her desk had to be clean as a whistle.

Ms. Rooney's class was going to make invitations for the kindergartners.

"Ready?" asked Ms. Rooney.

Dawn Bosco flew down the aisle. She slapped a piece of paper on Emily's eraser bits pile.

"Did you find that Pilgrim dress?" Emily asked.

Too late.

Dawn was halfway to the front of the room.

Alex Green came next. He slapped a box of crayons on top of the paper.

Emily opened the crayons.

Great. They were new and pointy.

Jill Simon raised her hand. She looked as if she was going to cry.

"I have horrible crayons," she said. "They're flat as pancakes."

Ms. Rooney sighed. "Give her a new box," she told Alex.

"Baby," Alex said.

Ms. Rooney frowned. "Are we all set now?"

Emily picked up a red crayon.

She was going to draw a leaf on the front.

It was much easier than drawing a turkey.

The inside was a snap. Everyone was writing the same thing:

PLEASE COME TO ROOM 113

THE DAY BEFORE THANKSGIVING.

WE ARE HAVING A FEAST.

Emily finished her card.

It was a little plain inside, she thought.

She tried to think of how to zip it up.

She took a pink crayon. She drew a picture of a baby in one corner.

She took a blue crayon. She drew a second baby in the other corner.

She thought about her own baby, the one who was coming any day now.

Almost everything was ready.

A yellow room with balloons painted in one corner.

Tiny white clothes in the drawers.

And another thing:

Emily had saved all her money in an old bubble bath bottle.

She was going to buy the baby its first toy. Something really special.

"Who wants to bring the invitations to the kindergarten?" Ms. Rooney asked.

Everyone raised a hand.

Everyone but Beast.

He was drawing a turkey galloping across his invitation.

A farmer with an ax was galloping after the turkey.

"This turkey's in trouble," he said.

Ms. Rooney looked around. "Emily, you'd better go. You know where the kindergarten is."

Emily smiled. It was her little sister Stacy's class.

"I know, too," Dawn said.

Ms. Rooney nodded.

Emily rushed around the room. She grabbed up a pile of invitations.

Dawn rushed, too.

They went down the hall.

"About the Pilgrim dress . . ." Emily began.

"Great dress," said Dawn. "I love it."

"Did you find it?" Emily asked.

Dawn shook her head. "Forgot to look."

They turned in at the kindergarten room.

Mrs. Zachary's class was sitting at tables.

They were rolling pieces of dough into long, skinny worms.

Mrs. Zachary smiled at them. "I think a surprise is coming," she told her class.

Emily looked around for Stacy. She wasn't at any of the tables.

"Would you like to give out the invitations?" Mrs. Zachary asked them.

They began to walk around the room.

Emily kept her own invitation on the bottom.

Stacy would love it.

She'd know why Emily had drawn the babies.

But Stacy wasn't there.

Emily rounded the fourth table.

Stacy *was* there.

She was bent over the table.

She was wearing an old white hat. It had rabbit ears.

It was left over from when she was three.

Emily leaned over her. "Why . . ." she began.

Stacy stuck out her lip.

Emily knew that meant "I'm not talking."

Emily handed her the invitation.

Mrs. Zachary was telling the class what the words meant.

Stacy looked at the pink and blue babies.

She put the invitation on the floor under her table.

"You have to go now," she told Emily. "I'm making a pretzel."

Emily went out the door.

She waited for Dawn to catch up.

"Why is Stacy wearing that dopey baby hat?" Dawn asked.

Emily raised her shoulders in the air.

She didn't have time to think about Stacy and rabbit hats right now.

She was trying to think about how to ask Dawn again for the Pilgrim dress.

Chapter 3

"**R**eady!" yelled Emily. "Get set . . ."
She wound the jump rope around her wrist. She began to turn.

This morning Emily was an ender. She didn't mind, though.

Jill was the other ender.

Emily could see that Jill *did* mind. Her fat cheeks were red as her bows.

Emily kept turning. At the same time she looked toward the kindergarten line.

She could see Stacy . . . wearing that rabbit hat again. The ears stuck up like feathers.

She looked more like a turkey than a rabbit.

Right now Dawn was jumping. "Faster," she told Emily.

Sometimes Dawn was fresh, Emily thought. Fresh as a fish.

She started to laugh. Fresh as a Fig Newton.

Just then Dawn tripped over the rope. She missed.

"Your fault, Emily," Dawn yelled. "You weren't going fast enough."

"I was so—" Emily remembered the Pilgrim dress and stopped.

"Take the end, Dawn," Sherri Dent yelled.

Dawn didn't move. "It's a do-over."

Linda Lorca put her hands on her hips. "Are we ever going to play?"

Dawn sniffed again.

She took the end of the rope.

At last it was Emily's turn.

She rocked back and forth on her sneakers. "Ready . . . set . . ."

She dived in.

At that moment Beast was racing across the school yard.

Matthew was right behind him.

"Run for your life," yelled Matthew.

Beast ran faster . . . right into Emily and the jump rope.

"Oof."

The rope whipped around Emily's leg.

Emily crashed into Dawn.

Dawn crashed into Sherri and Jill.

The bell rang.

Everyone limped inside.

Ms. Rooney met them at the door.

She was eating a banana sandwich. "Breakfast," she said.

Then she looked at Jill. "What's going on? Your elbow is bleeding."

"Really?" Jill began to cry.

"It's Beast's fault," Dawn said. "He didn't even look—"

"Tattletale," said Emily.

"Whoa." Ms. Rooney shook her head. "What happened to being nice to each other?"

Ms. Rooney closed her eyes.

The class knew what to do.

Everyone dashed for a seat.

Emily dashed the fastest. She shoved her books inside her desk.

She looked toward the front of the room.

Ms. Rooney opened her eyes. "Good start," she said. "But I think we should talk about something special this week."

"Ms. Rooney's Thanksgiving Feast," said Beast.

Emily smiled. *The new baby*, she wanted to say.

She didn't, though.

She looked out the window, thinking about names.

Stacy said she didn't care.

Emily cared. She was hoping for Caitlin for a girl. And something different for a boy. Connor, maybe.

"Someone's dreaming," Ms. Rooney said.

Emily looked up.

Ms. Rooney winked at her. "I know what you're dreaming about."

Everyone laughed.

Everyone else knew, too.

"This is November," said Ms. Rooney.

"Turkey time," said Matthew.

"Fig pudding," said Jill.

"Yucks," said everyone else.

"And a Good Neighbors Contest," said Ms. Rooney. "We have to find out what a good neighbor is."

Emily stopped thinking about the baby and turkey.

She loved contests.

She was going to find out about this one.

And then she was going to win.

She looked across at Dawn.

She knew what Dawn was thinking.

Dawn thought *she* was going to win.

Dawn looked back. She made a prune face at Emily.

Emily thought about the Pilgrim dress.

Too bad about the dress.

She scrunched up her nose. She made a prune face, too.

Chapter 4

It was Thursday, after school. Emily rattled around in the kitchen cabinets.

She could hear Stacy's footsteps.

She looked over her shoulder. "Aren't you hot in that hat?"

"No." Stacy shook her head.

"You look like . . ." Emily began. "A turkey. A big . . ."

"I do not," Stacy said. "What are you do-ing, anyway?"

"Looking for my apron." Emily slammed the drawer. "And I'm late. Very late."

"Behind the closet door," Stacy said.

Emily opened the door. She grabbed the apron off the hook.

It was an old one from Aunt Eileen, red with a couple of stains.

"You saved my life," she told Stacy.

Emily raced down the hall. She gave her mother a quick kiss. "I'm going to Sherri's."

"Me, too." Stacy reached for her jacket.

What would everyone say about that hat?

"No," Emily told her. "The class is making cranberry sauce for the Thanksgiving Feast."

Stacy stuck out her lip. She put her jacket back on the chair.

Emily thought about the Thanksgiving Feast and the Pilgrim dress.

She and Dawn hadn't talked to each other for two days. Not since they had made prune faces.

This afternoon she had to make up with Dawn . . . no matter what.

Emily went out the front door.

She stopped at the end of the path.

Stacy was at the window. She was twirling her hat strings.

She looked silly.

Emily took another step.

No, she looked sad.

Emily sighed. "Come on, Stacy," she called.

Stacy was out the door in two seconds. "You're my best friend, Emily," she said.

They raced toward Sherri's house.

Half the class was there ahead of them.

Mrs. Dent came down the hall. "I see you brought an apron," she told Emily.

"I brought one, too." Dawn held up a new apron. It was yellow with lace.

That Dawn.

Emily swallowed. "Great apron," she said.

"I brought an apron, too," said Beast. He waved a Kleenex in the air.

He tucked it in his shirt.

Everyone laughed.

"I don't have . . ." Stacy began.

"Don't worry." Mrs. Dent smiled. "I have tons of aprons."

They followed her into the kitchen.

Mrs. Dent tied an apron around Stacy's waist.

It dipped down almost to the floor.

Mrs. Dent put her hand on Stacy's chin. "Stacy reminds me of someone."

"Who?" Emily asked.

"I'm not sure," Mrs. Dent said.

Dawn began to talk about the contest. "I'm going to win." She looked at Emily.

Emily thought about the prize. It was a looks-like-gold medal that said GOOD NEIGHBOR.

If only she'd win.

Mrs. Dent put the chopper on the table.

"This is easy," she said. "All we have to do is wash the cranberries. Chop them up. Throw in an orange. Add a little sugar—"

"We even have Good Neighbors notebooks," Dawn said. "Every time we're good neighbors we put in a check."

"*Mazel tov*," said Mrs. Dent.

"That means 'good luck,' " Sherri said.

"Emily might win," Stacy said.

"Sure. The best good neighbor should win." Mrs. Dent brought a bowl of cranberries to the table. "Now throw out the bad ones."

She put her hands on her hips. "We don't

want cranberries that are shriveled up like raisins."

They leaned over the table.

Dawn leaned the hardest.

She took up the most room.

Emily wanted to give her a shove.

She remembered the dress just in time.

They picked through the berries.

Stacy helped pick, too.

She threw out a bunch of bad ones.

She threw out some good ones, too.

Emily wiggled her eyebrows at her to be careful.

"Now the chopper." Mrs. Dent looked serious. "Never put your hands inside. Use this wooden thing to press the berries down."

She dumped some cranberries into the top. "Someone can turn the wheel."

Sherri was closest. "Me first . . ."

"Some good neighbor," said Mrs. Dent.

"Oops," Sherri said.

"How about Stacy?" said Mrs. Dent.

Stacy began to turn. "Gobble gobble."

Emily gave her a nudge. "Don't act like a turkey."

"I'm not a turkey," Stacy said. "I'm a baby."

Emily felt her face get red. "This is the last time I'll ever . . ." she began.

Stacy closed her mouth.

They watched red cranberry meat and juice drip into a bowl.

Mrs. Dent chopped an orange. "We'll throw this in, too. Skin and all."

She looked at Emily. "You can do the sugar. A teeny tiny bit less than half a cup."

Emily poured out the sugar.

Everyone had a turn at the wheel.

Then they were finished. "Enough for the whole Thanksgiving Feast," Mrs. Dent said.

Emily tried to give Dawn a smile.

It was hard.

Dawn was trying to push her away from the end of the table.

Mrs. Dent clapped her hands. "I know who Stacy reminds me of."

Emily looked up. "Who?"

"Jill," said Mrs. Dent. "Jill Simon."

Emily looked at Jill.

She looked back at Stacy.

Jill always looked worried.

Usually Stacy didn't worry about anything.

Emily bit her lip. Mrs. Dent was right.

Stacy had the same look that Jill had.

Emily wondered why.

Chapter 5

Emily hung her jacket in the closet.
She went straight to her seat.

Today was an important day.

The class was going to work on next week's Thanksgiving Feast.

Ms. Rooney had drawn a picture on the chalkboard.

Emily thought it looked like a pumpkin.

No, it looked like . . .

What did it look like?

Ms. Rooney tapped her picture with chalk. "Guess what this is."

"A potato?" Jill asked.

Ms. Rooney laughed. "It's a plate. Underneath is a place mat. Next to the plate is . . ."

"A spoon. And a glass on top," said Emily.

Ms. Rooney had drawn a napkin next to the plate.

It looked like a crooked little triangle.

"Today we'll draw place mats. I'll give out paper. And Alex . . ."

Alex stood up. He began to pass crayons around.

Emily looked over toward Dawn.

She thought about the Thanksgiving costume.

She sighed. Her mother had told her to wear her yellow pajamas.

"Yes," said her father. "Be a nice corn-on-the-cob. They had corn at the first Thanksgiving."

Emily hadn't answered. She'd die before she'd wear those lumpy pajamas in front of everyone.

At last Alex dumped crayons on her desk.

This time the box was old and ripped.

Half the crayons were broken.

Who cared?

The brown one was great. So were the red and orange.

She was going to draw a whole Thanksgiving dinner.

A fat turkey.

Tan stuffing.

Red cranberry sauce.

Cut-up carrots.

Nothing to it.

She looked across at Dawn.

Dawn was leaning over her desk.

She was sneaking some of her lunch.

It was Emily's favorite. Chicken with grapes.

Emily's mouth watered.

She felt like making a fish face at Dawn.

She didn't, though.

She thought about her new Good Neighbors notebook.

It was inside her desk.

She had given herself two checks already.

She had picked up a piece of paper from under Linda Lorca's desk.

She had let Jill in front of her in line.

Too bad she hadn't said "thank you," to Alex Green for the crayons.

That would have been three.

Right now she smiled at Dawn.

That was number three.

She didn't wait to see if Dawn was surprised.

She took the hall pass.

She went outside for a quick drink.

She stopped at the kindergarten door.

Stacy was staring out the window.

She was wearing the white hat. She was sucking her thumb.

Emily frowned.

Last night Stacy had had a nightmare.

She had cried and cried.

Emily had heard their mother rushing into the room.

Just then someone came up behind Emily.

It was Dawn.

"I wanted to tell you something," Dawn said. "I'm going to lend you my Pilgrim dress."

Emily took a deep breath. She couldn't believe it. "That's wonderful."

She remembered to say "thank you."

It would be her fourth check.

Dawn nodded. "I think I can give myself five checks for this. It's *really* being a good neighbor."

Emily swallowed.

That Dawn.

"Thank you," Emily said again. "But I'm wearing something else."

"Really?"

"Yes," said Emily. "I'm wearing a corn costume."

She rushed down the hall toward the girls' room. "It's yellow. It almost looks like pajamas."

Chapter 6

Emily lay on her bedroom floor.
She reached under the bed.

Dust was underneath. So was the old bubble bath bottle.

Emily rolled it out.

The money inside made a nice clinking sound.

Stacy sat down next to her. "Is that money for a Christmas present?" she asked.

Emily shook her head.

She smiled at Stacy. "It's for a birthday present."

Stacy smiled, too.

"I'm going to the store right now," Emily said. "Want to come?"

Stacy frowned a little. "You want me to come with you?"

"Sure," Emily said. "Why not?"

"Hmm," Stacy said. She went down the hall for her jacket.

Emily stood there waiting for her.

She had a warm feeling inside her chest.

It had been a wonderful day.

All day she had thought about the present she'd buy for the baby.

She'd thought of a rattle, something that would make a soft noise.

Or maybe it should be something that would hang in the yellow room.

Something for the baby to look at when she went to sleep.

Or when *he* went to sleep.

At last Stacy was ready. "I'll wait outside," she said. She yanked at the front door.

Emily went down the hall.

Her mother was in the kitchen.

Emily held up the bubble bath bottle.

Her mother stretched a little and smiled. "Time to buy the baby a toy?"

Emily nodded.

Emily's mother nodded, too. "It's going to be soon. A real Thanksgiving baby."

Outside, Stacy was jumping in the leaves.

She had crumpled-up leaves on her jacket and in her rabbit-ears hat.

"Look, Emily," she said. "All the leaves are off the trees."

"I can't wait for snow," Emily said.

"I can't wait for my birthday," Stacy said.

Emily stopped. "Right. The beginning of December."

She had forgotten all about it.

She and Stacy walked to Linden Avenue.

They passed Beast and Matthew on the way.

The boys were leaning over, eating ice pops.

The pops were dripping all over the sidewalk.

Emily shivered. It was much too cold for ice pops.

Emily spotted Dawn Bosco.

She was halfway down the next street, coming toward them.

"Come on," Emily told Stacy. "Let's go."

They turned in at Kids' World.

"My favorite place," Stacy said.

They stopped at the counter. "Look," said Stacy. "Turkey pins."

Emily picked one up. It was a perfect pin to put on a jacket or a blouse.

It had perfect Thanksgiving colors.

"No good," said Stacy. "I can't wear a turkey for my December birthday."

Emily frowned. "What do you mean?"

Just then Dawn came in the door.

"Let's go in the back," Emily told Stacy.

"That's just the baby stuff," Stacy said. "We don't want to look at that."

"Yes, we do," said Emily. "That's why we're here."

She hurried down the aisle, away from Stacy. Away from Dawn.

In the back were rattles, and stuffed bears, and balls.

And then Emily saw it. The perfect present.

It was hanging on a cord.

It looked like a raindrop.

Emily closed her eyes.

She could see it in the baby's room.

She could see the baby watching it.

It would sparkle in the sunlight.

At night it would catch the light from the little lamp.

She reached for it.

Someone was in back of her. "Look, Stacy," she said.

It wasn't Stacy.

It was Dawn.

"I wanted to tell you," Dawn began. Her face was red. "I want you to wear the Pilgrim dress."

Emily began to shake her head.

It was almost as if Dawn knew what she was thinking.

"It's not because of the contest," Dawn said slowly. "I was thinking about what Ms. Rooney said. You know . . . about finding out what a good neighbor is."

Emily took a breath.

"Don't say no," Dawn said.

Emily laughed. "Don't worry, I won't."

Just then Stacy came down the aisle. "How are you going to find my birthday present in with this stuff?"

"It's your birthday?" Dawn asked.

Emily shook her head. "No. This is for the new baby's birthday."

Stacy opened her mouth.

Her face turned red.

"I'm sick of that baby," she said.

She rushed out the door.

Emily took a last look at the hanging raindrop. Then she raced out the door in back of Stacy.

Chapter 7

"Excuse me," Beast yelled. "Coming through."

Beast had a bowl of shiny apples on his head.

Emily jumped out of his way.

She didn't jump fast enough.

"Yeow," Beast yelled.

Apples rolled down the aisle and under the desk.

Everyone helped to pick them up.

They were all trying to be good neighbors.

It was Tuesday, the day before Ms. Rooney's Thanksgiving Feast.

Everyone was rushing around.

Desks had to be cleaned.

Windowsills had to be dusted.

The class had drawn about a million turkeys.

They were hanging all over the place.

Right now Emily crawled around under the desks.

She reached for a couple of apples.

She brought them to the table at the side of the room.

The table was filled with food.

Little cups with nuts and raisins.

Fat pears and purple grapes.

More food was in the cafeteria refrigerator.

The class had made applesauce and cut celery.

Ms. Rooney clapped her hands. "Seats, please," she called.

Emily slid into her seat.

Up in front Ms. Rooney was trying to fix her puffy brown hair. "Whew," she said. "What a busy day."

She looked around at the class. "I think the Good Neighbors Contest has worked."

Emily looked around, too.

Ms. Rooney was right. Everyone was trying.

Almost everybody.

"I forgot." Beast clapped his head. "I have only two checks."

Emily pulled out her book. She began to count.

Forty-two checks.

She wondered if it would be enough to win.

Ms. Rooney walked up and down. She collected the books.

"I'll count these up tonight," she said. "We'll see who gets the medal tomorrow."

Emily looked up at the Good Neighbor medal.

It was hanging on the bulletin board.

It reminded her of something—the beautiful hanging raindrop for the baby.

Emily felt a tiny knot of worry.

She hoped the raindrop was still at the store.

She hadn't bought it the other day.

She had rushed out after Stacy.

She had . . .

"Emily?" Ms. Rooney asked.

Emily jumped.

"I was telling the class," said Ms. Rooney, "because everyone has worked so hard—"

Beast slid down in his seat. "I'm worn out," he said.

Ms. Rooney laughed. "Me, too."

She looked toward the door. "Another surprise is coming," she said.

The door opened. The cafeteria lady poked her head in. "Is this the right time?"

"Perfect," said Ms. Rooney.

She smiled at the class. "I made candy apples for everyone last night."

Emily's mouth watered.

"You can take them home," said Ms. Rooney. She winked. "A special before-Thanksgiving treat."

Just then the bell rang.

Emily went to the front of the room.

She took Dawn's Pilgrim dress with one hand.

She held the candy apple in the other.

Everyone else had both hands filled, too.

Beast had his Pilgrim father suit in one hand. He had a brown Pilgrim father beard in the other. His candy apple was in his mouth.

Emily went out the door and down the hall.

She should be happy, she thought. She should be excited.

It was almost Thanksgiving. It was time for the feast.

The new baby was coming.

She felt sad, though. Sad about Stacy.

Stacy always looked sad now. And Emily didn't know why.

Emily thought back to the morning at Kids' World.

Stacy had run outside. She had raced down the street.

She wouldn't wait for Emily.

"I'm going to get something for your birth-day, too," Emily kept calling.

But Stacy hadn't looked back.

She hadn't talked to Emily for the rest of the morning.

Chapter 8

Emily climbed up the back steps.

She was glad to be home.

Her arms were tired from holding everything.

The back door was locked.

She peered in the window.

No lights.

A bunch of stuff on the kitchen table—a bag of flour, olives, a couple of cinnamon sticks.

Her mother must be getting ready for their own Thanksgiving feast.

Emily banged on the kitchen door.

She could hear Stacy's cat, Pest, meowing.

She took another look.

Pest was curled up on her mother's old sweater.

She banged again.

No one was home.

She reached under her collar for her key.

It wasn't there.

She shook her head.

She remembered she had taken the key off when she'd had her bath.

It was probably still on the edge of the tub.

Emily sank down on the top step.

Everyone had forgotten her.

Some good neighbors.

The sun had gone in. The sky looked gray.

It was windy and cold.

Emily leaned over to take a bite of the apple.

She had to be careful.

She didn't want to get anything on Dawn's Pilgrim dress.

She took another bite. A piece of candy broke off.

After a minute an ant rushed across the step to grab it.

Next door she heard a bang.

Mrs. Miles, their neighbor, had opened her door.

"Emily," she said, "I've been looking and looking for you. I don't know how you sneaked past me."

"I didn't—"

Mrs. Miles waved her hand. "No matter. Come on over. I'm going to take care of you. Give you dinner."

Emily looked around for somewhere to put the rest of her apple.

She'd give it to the ants.

She leaned over.

The apple rolled off the stick and across the collar of the Pilgrim dress.

Emily stared at it—a round dark spot on the silky material.

"Your mother went to the hospital," said Mrs. Miles. "To have the baby."

Emily looked up.

"No, not yet," said Mrs. Miles. "Maybe not until tonight. But hurry. It's getting cold."

Emily ran across to Mrs. Miles's kitchen.

Inside, it was warm and bright.

Steam was coming from the teakettle.

"Where's Stacy?" Emily asked.

"At the hospital, too." Mrs. Miles poured

milk into the tea—so much milk there was almost no tea. "Your grandmother is there, and your father."

Emily remembered to say "thank you." Thank you for the tea, for the chicken, for the string beans.

She felt like crying.

Everyone was over at the hospital.

Soon the new baby would be born.

And she was the only one who wouldn't be there.

Mrs. Miles had hung the gray Pilgrim dress in the doorway.

It was a mess.

If only her mother were there to tell her what to do.

"What's the matter, Emily?" Mrs. Miles asked.

Emily shook her head.

Mrs. Miles smiled. "When my baby brother was born, I was sad, too."

Emily looked up.

"I thought my mother and my two sisters wouldn't love me as much. I thought they'd have much more fun with the new baby."

"No . . ." Emily began. "I don't . . ." She closed her mouth.

There was too much to explain.

But Mrs. Miles had just told her something —something important.

Emily reached for another piece of cake.

Mrs. Miles was still looking at her.

Emily knew she had to say something.

"You're a good neighbor," she told Mrs. Miles. "A really good neighbor."

Chapter 9

Emily was dreaming about something.
It was a bits and pieces dream. It was about walking down Stone Street, which turned into Linden Street, which . . .

She opened her eyes.

She could see Stacy in the bed across the room.

Then she remembered. Her grandmother and Stacy had come home after dinner.

The baby still hadn't been born.

Emily closed her eyes. The dream began again.

In the dream someone was pulling on her arm.

"Stop that," she said.

The dream person didn't stop. It was pulling at her shoulders, laughing.

"You have to wake up," it said in a voice just like her father's.

"No." Emily tried to shake her head.

Then she heard Stacy.

She opened her eyes.

The lights were on in the bedroom.

The dream person really was her father.

"Wake up, old Emily," he said. "I have the best news you've ever heard."

Emily sat up.

In the other bed Stacy was sitting up, too.

"Is it morning?" Emily asked.

She looked outside. Everything was dark and still—everything except a circle of yellow from the streetlight.

She caught her breath.

"It's the middle of the night," her father said. "Two o'clock in the morning."

He was smiling, waiting for them to be really awake.

"It's the baby," Emily said.

Her father nodded. His eyes were shiny, almost as if he had tears in them.

Emily reached out to hug him. "Tell us. Hurry."

"It's Caitlin," her father said.

"A girl," Emily said.

She was smiling now, too. She could see a little baby girl in the yellow room.

She could see her reaching out.

"A sister," she said. She loved the sound of it.

"We'll take her for walks," she told Stacy.

The baby would love their old trains, their old dolls.

"Caitlin," she said.

"We'll call her Katie," said her father.

Emily looked across at Stacy.

Stacy was leaning back against her pillow.

Her hair was in her eyes.

She wasn't smiling.

She looked as if she was going to cry.

Emily thought about being at Mrs. Miles's house this afternoon.

She knew what was the matter with Stacy.

Her father was still talking. "She weighs seven pounds," he said. "She has a little brown hair. And she looks just like you and Stacy."

"No, she doesn't," said Stacy.

Emily wanted to say something.

She was too sleepy, though.

She sank down under the covers. She could hardly keep her eyes open.

Just before she fell asleep, she remembered the Pilgrim dress. She thought about the raindrop for the baby. And she thought about Stacy.

She knew how she was going to fix everything.

Tomorrow.

She was a big sister now.

A big sister twice.

Chapter 10

Emily sat at one edge of her seat.

Stacy sat on the other edge.

Ms. Rooney was serving turkey to everyone.

Mrs. Dent was walking around with the cranberry sauce.

Emily reached for Stacy's hand.

"I want to tell you . . ." she began.

Stacy looked up.

"When I was at Mrs. Miles's house yester-day, I was thinking about you."

Stacy snorted. "I had to sit in a brown kind of room at the hospital. I couldn't even watch something good on TV. News, news, news. That's what everyone was watching."

Emily laughed a little. "I wished you were there at Mrs. Miles's," she told Stacy. "I love being your big sister."

Stacy didn't say anything for a moment.

Then she sighed. "I think you'll love Caitlin more."

"I didn't know you were worried about that," Emily said. "Not until yesterday."

Emily reached for Stacy's turkey hat. "You don't need to be a baby."

Emily put the hat inside her desk. "I love you," she said. "Just as much as I love Katie. You don't have to be a baby."

Stacy nodded a little.

"Besides," Emily said, "you're going to have fun being a big sister now."

"I never thought of that," Stacy said.

Emily gave her a little tap. "Start thinking now."

Dawn came by. She put celery on their plates.

"I love the turkey pin," she said.

Emily closed her eyes for a moment.

This morning she had raced to the store. She had bought the pin.

It had covered the spot on the dress.

She had a little money left.

She would take the dress to the dry cleaner's this afternoon.

She had told Dawn the whole thing.

"You're a good neighbor," Dawn had said, and grinned. "I'll lend you the pin sometime."

Emily took a sip of her apple juice.

There was no money left for the baby's raindrop.

It was all right, though.

She was going to play with Caitlin every single day.

That was the important thing.

Up in front Ms. Rooney clapped her hands.

"Isn't it lovely?" she said. "All of us here together."

"It really is Thanksgiving," said Mrs. Dent.

"Good neighbors together," said Ms. Rooney.

She reached for the medal.

"Do you know what I was thinking?" she said.

The class waited.

"I think you all deserve the medal."

"Me, too," said Beast.

"Suppose we leave it there—right on the bulletin board for all of us."

Emily looked at the medal.

She looked at Dawn.

They smiled at each other.

It was perfect.

Stacy was smiling, too. "A big sister," she said.

Emily took a bite of turkey.

Her grandmother was home cooking. "No trouble for me to make the turkey," she said. "I must have cooked a hundred of them."

Emily thought of her mother coming home tomorrow.

She thought of the baby looking just like her and Stacy.

She leaned across the aisle toward Dawn.

"Happy Thanksgiving," she said.

TURKEY TIME

. . .

Polk Street Thanksgiving Treats

Contents

Matthew's Mayflower Mat and Napkin Rings

You will need:

2 sheets 9-by-12-inch construction paper
—one orange, one brown
scissors
ruler
pencil

PLACE MAT

Then:

1. Place the orange sheet in front of you.

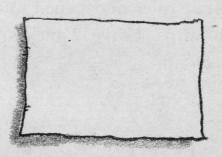

2. Use your ruler and pencil to mark 12 one-inch strips.

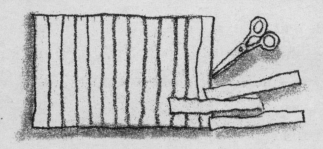

3. Cut these strips.
4. Place the brown sheet in front of you.
5. Fold it in half.
6. Turn the paper so the fold is on the bottom.
7. Use your ruler and pencil to mark 9 one-inch strips. Leave 2 inches on the nonfolded end.

8. Cut these slits. Start cutting from the folded end.

9. Keep paper folded. Use your scissors to make fringe. Cut on the nonfolded end. Be sure to leave some space between the fringe and the slits.

10. Open up the brown paper.

11. Take 7 orange strips and weave them through the brown slits.

NAPKIN RING

You can make a napkin ring, too. Use the extra orange strips.

1. Make a strip into a circle and staple.
2. Open up a napkin. Pull the napkin through the ring.

3. Straighten the napkin after it's pulled through.

Derrick Grace's Turkey Place Cards

You will need:

A pine cone. It should be about the size
of your fist.

2 pipe cleaners

brown or black marker

construction paper

scissors

glue

Then:

1. Cut one pipe cleaner in half.

2. Make the two pieces into two turkey
feet.

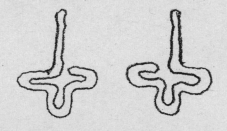

3. Place the pine cone on its side. The fat end will be the back.

4. Press the feet between two spaces on either side of the pine cone. Glue.

5. Cut the other pipe cleaner in half. (You will use only one of the halves.) Make one piece into a turkey head. Use your marker to make eyes.

6. Press the head between two spaces in the front of the pine cone.

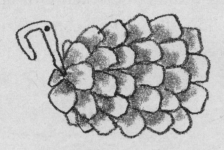

7. Draw 3 feathers on construction paper. Use any colors you wish. Yellow, orange, and red are good choices. Make the feathers large enough to write the person's name.

8. Cut out the feathers. Write the person's name on one feather.

9. Press the feathers in a fan-like shape between the spaces in back of the pine cone. Be sure the feather with the person's name is in the middle. Glue.

10. Let the glue dry. Put the turkey on its feet. You may have to bend the feet so the turkey will stand without your help.

The turkey place card should be placed at the top center of your place mat.

Noah's Nutty Turkey Centerpiece

You will need:

1 sheet of 9-by-12-inch brown construction paper

small pieces of yellow and red construction paper

black marker

glue

pie tin

paper plate

crayons

jar of peanuts

large box of raisins

package of walnuts

a few red or yellow leaves

Then:

1. Fold the brown construction paper in half the short way.

2. Draw a wave-like shape from the edge of the fold.

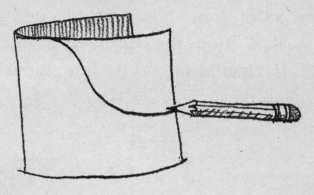

3. Cut on the line.
4. Open the larger piece. Join the ends to make a circle.

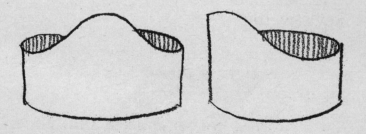

5. Make turkey eyes with your marker.

6. Draw a small triangle on the yellow sheet of paper . . . small enough for a beak. Cut out the triangle and fold it in half. Open it up a little and glue it onto the turkey.

7. Draw a long tear-drop shape on the red piece of paper. This will be the turkey's wattle.

8. Cut the tear drop. Place it under the beak.

9. Glue it to the turkey.

10. Color the edges of the paper plate. This will be the turkey's tail.

11. Staple the plate to the back of the turkey. The colored side should face the back of the turkey's head.

12. Place the turkey in the center of a pie tin. Pour the peanuts and raisins inside the body. Put walnuts and colored leaves around the edges of the pie tin.

Sherri's Table Setting

Matthew's mat goes on the bottom.

The plate is in the center.

The knife and spoon go to the right. Make sure the sharp side of the knife is facing the plate.

(Hint: 5 letters in *knife* and *spoon* . . .

5 letters in *right)*

The fork goes to the left.

(Hint: 4 letters in *fork* . . .

4 letters in *left)*

The napkin can go next to the fork, or on the plate.

The glass is on top, between the plate and knife.

Beast's Best Manners

BEAST SAYS: Keep your napkin in your lap.

MATTHEW SAYS: But don't forget to use it.

BEAST SAYS: Chew with your mouth closed.

MATTHEW SAYS: And don't talk when your mouth is full.

BEAST SAYS: Don't play with your food.

MATTHEW SAYS: No races with peas, no hiding spinach under the plate.

BEAST SAYS: *Ask* for the salt, pepper, and butter.

MATTHEW SAYS: Don't climb across the table to get them.

BEAST SAYS: Cut your food into bite-size pieces . . . not all at once, but when you're ready for the next one.

MATTHEW SAYS: Bite size doesn't mean a hippopotamus-size bite.

BEAST SAYS: Take the nearest piece of cake . . .

MATTHEW SAYS: even if it's as small as an ant.

BEAST SAYS: When you're finished, leave the knife and fork on the dinner plate . . . leave your spoon on the dessert plate.

MATTHEW SAYS: And ask to be excused.

Timothy's Turkey Treats
(Serves two people)

BEAST SAYS: *Don't forget to wash your hands first . . .*
MS. ROONEY SAYS: *. . . with soap.*

You will need:
    1 ¹/₂ cups of leftover turkey
    8 grapes
    12 raisins (6 for the salad, 6 to eat now)
    a few chopped walnuts or pecans
    a few chunks of celery if you like them
    1 tablespoon of mayonnaise
    2 or 3 small pieces of torn lettuce
    salt and pepper
    2 pita pockets

Then:

1. Shred the turkey with your fingers.
2. Add everything else.
3. Mix until the mayonnaise coats every-thing.
4. Stuff the mix into two pockets.

Mrs. Dent's Cranberry Creation
(Serves two people)

MS. ROONEY SAYS: *It's easy to cut fingers and chop thumbs. Ask an adult to help.*

You will need:

1 cup of cranberries

1 orange

$1/2$ cup of sugar, or a little more to taste

Then:

1. Wash the cranberries.
2. Throw away any stems or wrinkled ones.
3. Cut the orange into 4 pieces.
4. Pull away about half the peel and throw away.

5. Use a blender or grinder to chop the cranberries and oranges.

6. Pour in the sugar and mix.

7. Cover and store in the refrigerator.

Sherri Dent's Cranberry Concoction
(Serves two people)

MS. ROONEY SAYS: *Don't try this recipe alone. The stove gets hot . . . and the cranberries, too!*

BEAST SAYS: *What's a concoction anyway?*

You will need:

    1 cup of cranberries

    $^1/_2$ cup of water

    $^1/_2$ cup of sugar, or a little more to taste

Then:

    1. Wash the cranberries.

    2. Throw away any stems or wrinkled ones.

    3. Put the cranberries, water, and sugar in a pot.

    4. Cook uncovered over medium heat.

5. When the mixture begins to boil, lower the heat.

6. It is finished when the berries split. It will be slightly thickened. Cool in the refrigerator.

Dawn Bosco's Red Pepper Corn
(Serves two people)

MS. ROONEY SAYS: *Remember to get help cutting the tomato and pepper. Remember, too, the lids of cans are sharp. Ask someone to open the can for you.*

You will need:
  1 ripe tomato
  1 small can of corn
  $1/4$ red pepper

Then:
  1. Carefully cut a tomato in half.
  2. With a spoon, scoop out the insides. (Eat them if you wish.)
  3. Open the can of corn. At the sink, pour the corn into a strainer. Let the liquid drain away.

4. Cut the pepper into small chunks.

5. Mix the corn and pepper together.

6. Spoon into the tomato.

7. Some corn and pepper mix may be left over. You can save it for dinner.

8. Store in the refrigerator.

Linda Lorca's Ladyfingers
(serves two people)

MS. ROONEY SAYS: *Bananas slice easily. You don't need a sharp knife. Use a table knife, or even the back of a spoon.*

You will need:
- 2 ripe bananas
- 3 ladyfingers
- 2 heaping tablespoons of whipped topping
- 2 cherries, if you wish

Then:

1. Press pieces of the ladyfingers into two cups or small bowls.

2. Slice the bananas.

3. In a bowl, mix the bananas and whipped topping together. Be sure to do this gently.

4. Spoon the mixture into the cup. Put the cherry on top.

5. Chill in the refrigerator for an hour or two.

Polk Street Pilgrims' Punch
(Serves two people)

You will need:

1 quart of apple cider

2 scoops of vanilla ice cream

cinnamon or nutmeg to sprinkle

2 cinnamon sticks

Then:

1. Put a scoop of ice cream into each of two tall glasses.

2. Slowly fill the glasses with apple cider and stir.

3. Sprinkle the cinnamon or nutmeg over the tops.

4. Put a cinnamon stick in each glass.